THE NOTEBOOK OF DOOM

BATTLE OF THE BOSS-MONSTER

by Troy Cummings

BRANCHES

SCHOLASTIC INC.

HAVE YOU READ ALL OF THE NOTEBOOK OF DOOM BOOKS?

#1 Rise of the Balloon Goons

#2 Day of the Night Crawlers

#3 Attack of the Shadow Smashers

#4 Chomp of the Meat-Eating Vegetables

#5 Whack of the P-Rex

#6 Pop of the Bumpy Mummy

#7 Flurry of the Snombies

#8 Charge of the Lightning Bugs

#9 Rumble of the Coaster Ghost

#10 Snap of the Super-Goop

#11 Sneeze of the Octo-Schnozz

#12 March of the Vanderpants

#13 Battle of the Boss-Monster

COLLECT THEM ALL!

TABLE OF CONTENTS

To Penny and Harvey: I thought I asked you to stay out of trouble!

Thank you, Katie and Liz and Sam and Jessica and Kay and Kirk, for all your hard work, talent, patience, and humor—times thirteen!

Copyright © 2018 by Troy Cummings

All rights reserved. Published by Scholastic Inc., *Publishers since 1920*. SCHOLASTIC, BRANCHES, and associated logos are trademarks and/or registered trademarks of Scholastic Inc.

The publisher does not have any control over and does not assume any responsibility for author or third-party websites or their content.

No part of this publication may be reproduced, stored in a retrieval system, or transmitted in any form or by any means, electronic, mechanical, photocopying, recording, or otherwise, without written permission of the publisher. For information regarding permission, write to Scholastic Inc., Attention: Permissions Department, 557 Broadway, New York, NY 10012.

This book is a work of fiction. Names, characters, places, and incidents are either the product of the author's imagination or are used fictitiously, and any resemblance to actual persons, living or dead, business establishments, events, or locales is entirely coincidental.

Library of Congress Cataloging-in-Publication Data

Names: Cummings, Troy, author. | Cummings, Troy.
Notebook of doom ; 13.Title: Battle of the boss-monster / by Troy Cummings.
Description: First edition. | New York : Branches/Scholastic Inc., 2018. | Series: The Notebook of Doom ; 13
Summary: In the year since Alexander and his father moved to Stermont, he and his friends in the Super Secret Monster Patrol of Stermont Elementary have defeated all kinds of monsters, but now they face their greatest challenge, the boss-monster who has kidnapped fellow monster fighter Ms. Vanderpants and stolen the Notebook of Doom—and they have to do it before Alexander turns eight and stops being able to see monsters.
Identifiers: LCCN 2017032544| ISBN 9781338034561 (pbk.) | ISBN 9781338034578 (hardcover)
Subjects: LCSH: Monsters—Juvenile fiction. | Elementary schools—Juvenile fiction. | Friendship—Juvenile fiction. | Birthdays—Juvenile fiction. | Fathers and sons—Juvenile fiction. | Horror tales. | CYAC: Horror stories. | Monsters—Fiction. | Schools—Fiction. | Friendship—Fiction. | Birthdays—Fiction. | Fathers and sons—Fiction. | LCGFT: Horror fiction.
Classification: LCC PZ7.C91494 Bat 2018 | DDC 813.6 [Fic] —dc23 LC record available at https://lccn.loc.gov/2017032544

10 9 8 7 6 5 4 3 2 1   18 19 20 21 22

Printed in China   38
First edition, January 2018

Edited by Katie Carella
Book design by Liz Frances

A YEAR IN STERMONT

Alexander's dad grinned up at the calendar on the wall.

"Look at that, kiddo!" he said. "It's been one year since we moved to this kooky town!"

Alexander rinsed out his cereal bowl. "Kooky?" he asked.

FEBRUARY

1 year in Stermont!

29 LEAP DAY!

"Yeah, you know," his dad said. "There's always weird stuff happening here in Stermont — flat tires, strange weather, power outages."

Those were all monster attacks — balloon goons, snombies, and zapper-bugs! thought Alexander.

"Speaking of weird stuff . . ." his dad said. "Not every kid has a birthday once every four years. That's why I'm throwing you the weirdest birthday party ever tomorrow!"

He handed Alexander an invitation.

Put on your finest lampshade and come to

ALEXANDER BOPP'S
WEIRD BIRTHDAY PARTY!

8

* **When:** February 29.
* **When:** Leap day!
* **When:** 4:58 p.m.
* **Where:** 55 Jackdaw Street.

The exact minute Alexander was born!

2

"I've already invited your friends Rip and Nikki," said Alexander's dad. "Feel free to invite anyone else!" He stuffed a stack of invitations into Alexander's backpack.

"Jeez, dad," said Alexander. "I don't —"

BLUBRRBRRBBRRR!!

Alexander was interrupted by a low rumbling noise coming from outside. It sounded like a giant whoopee cushion.

A monster! he thought. He started for the door.

"Al, wait!" yelled his dad. "Don't forget your lunch." He tossed Alexander his lunch box. "I packed your favorite treat!"

"Triple-power-pucker pickles?" asked Alexander.

"Precisely!" said his dad. "Oh, and be sure to share them with Rip and Nikki!"

BLUBRRBRRBBRRR!! The noise outside was even louder.

"Okay!" said Alexander. *Unless they're already monster-chow!*

2 PUCKER UP!

BLUBRRBRRBBRRR!

Alexander raced toward the splattery sound in the woods. He jogged along logs and jumped over stumps until he came to an old, broken-down caboose.

Cracked glass

Dead vines

Hole in the wall

S.S.M.P.

S.S.M.P. = Super Secret Monster Patrol

The Super Secret Monster Patrol was a group of monster-fighters sworn to protect Stermont. Alexander was the leader. This caboose was their headquarters.

CLACK! A hatch on the roof flew open, and the two other club members popped out.

NIKKI HUBBARD
Hero in a hoodie.

SUPER SECRET: Nikki is actually a good monster, called a **JAMPIRE.**

Eats red juicy stuff.   Avoids sunlight.   Sees in the dark.

RIP BONKOWSKI
Bully with a heart of ~~gold,~~ ~~silver,~~ bronze.

SUPER SECRET: Rip is actually a good monster, called a **KNUCKLE-FISTED PUNCH-SMASHER.**

Eats sweets to transform into monster-mode!

Communicates with ant-monsters called **GI-NORM-ANTS.**

Bright blue spots

Clicky antennae

Razor-sharp mandibles

"Watch out, Salamander!" Nikki shouted, calling Alexander by his nickname. "The monster is coming your way!"

Alexander turned to see a big purple monster barreling toward him.

The monster bowled into Alexander, knocking him over. It leapt onto his chest and licked him. Thirty-nine times.

"Yechh!" Alexander yechhed. He was drenched in slobber. "This monster is a purple slurper! It's got thirty-nine tongues, and loves to lick stuff!"

"Yeah," said Nikki. "It slurped half the paint off our caboose!"

"How do we stop it?" Rip shouted.

Alexander had an idea. He squirmed against the squishy, purple tongues as he reached into his backpack. He flipped open his lunch box.

A sour vinegar smell cut through the air.

FWORP! Alexander jammed a triple-power-pucker pickle into one of the monster's many mouths.

GACK! The purple slurper's tongues flailed like frightened snakes.

MRRPHH!! The big tongue-tied monster made thirty-nine sour faces, then flopped off into the woods.

"Next time, lick on somebody your own size!" Rip shouted.

Nikki rushed to help Alexander to his feet. His shoes squished as he stood up.

"That was strange," said Alexander. "Slurpers normally live under dinner tables."

"So why's this one in the woods?" asked Nikki.

"I don't know," replied Alexander. "I just wish I could update the monster notebook."

"Yeah," said Rip, "but the dumb old boss-monster swiped it."

S.S.M.P.

SUBJECT
DOOM!

Beat-up old notebook filled with monster facts.

The S.S.M.P.'s super-secret weapon!

Now in the claws of the horrible boss-monster (whoever she is).

STOLEN!

THE TERRIBLE, MYSTERIOUS

BOSS-MONSTER!
WHO IS SHE?

?

"Don't forget that the boss-monster stole our principal, too!" said Nikki.

MS. VANDERPANTS
Cranky principal.
SUPER SECRET: Ms. Vanderpants is actually a good monster, called a **NAR-MADILLO.**

Armored shell

Pointy horn

KIDNAPPED!

"We need to find this big boss-monster and show her who's boss!" said Rip.

"Sure," said Alexander, "if only we knew where to look."

"Let's start with the one grown-up in town who can see monsters," said Nikki.

"Good idea!" said Alexander. "School's about to start. I bet he's already hiding under his desk!"

3 PRINCIPAL HOARSELY

Look!" said Alexander, as the friends jogged to school. "The purple slurper isn't the only monster out today."

There were signs of monsters everywhere.

Rusty!

Knotted!

The three friends ran a little faster and soon arrived at school.

"Weird," said Nikki. "There has never been a guard out front before."

"Move along, toddlers!" said the guard. "No funny business!"

"That's Ms. Sargent — from the Stermont Museum," Rip whispered as they passed through an x-ray scanner. "She's tougher than P-rex teeth!"

"Mr. Hoarsely must've hired her," Alexander said.

"He's really taking this security stuff seriously," said Nikki.

"Well, he *did* watch Vanderpants get nabbed by a monster," said Rip.

"*That* is exactly why we need to talk to him," said Alexander. "Come on!"

The friends rode the escalators up to the thirteenth floor.

The door to the principal's office was closed. Alexander knocked.

"Eep!"

"Open up, Hoarsely!" Rip yelled.

"Forget it!" the shaky voice called back. "It is too dangerous out there!"

Alexander leaned toward the door, and spoke calmly. "It's about Principal Vanderpants."

The door swung open, and Mr. Hoarsely waved them in. He wore a baggy suit that made him look like a half-stuffed scarecrow.

"Did you find her?" he asked.

"Not yet," said Nikki.

Mr. Hoarsely's shoulders drooped, making his jacket look even baggier. "We need her," he said. "Ms. Vanderpants was the S.S.M.P.'s best monster-fighter."

Rip's jaw dropped. "What?! Vanderpants was in the Monster Patrol?"

"Well, sure," said Mr. Hoarsely. "The S.S.M.P. was her idea. She created the notebook."

"No way!" said Alexander.

"Yes way," said Mr. Hoarsely.

"But . . . how?" asked Nikki.

Mr. Hoarsely looked out the window as he spoke.

I met Helen Vanderpants when I was just a kid. I was playing in Derwood Park when a cheese-blaster attacked me.

I was so scared that my black hair turned bright white!

But then Helen showed up. She transformed . . .

. . . and saved me! I've been by her side ever since.

I joined her club—the S.S.M.P.—and we battled monsters together for a while. But later, the S.S.M.P. disbanded. Then Helen became a principal so she could protect the kids of Stermont—and look for new monster-fighters.

That's how Ms. Vanderpants found you, Alexander. She has had her eye on you since the day you moved to Stermont.

She was pleased that you re-started the S.S.M.P. She even gave you one-on-one lessons to test you — to see if you were ready to help her battle the big boss.

"Now I *am* ready!" said Alexander. "Except. We can't *find* the boss-monster. We've searched everywhere!"

"Not everywhere . . ." Mr. Hoarsely jingled a keychain that said MS. VDP.

4 THE BIRTHDAY RULE

On the day Ms. Vanderpants got snatched," said Mr. Hoarsely, "she'd been driving around, looking for the boss-monster."

Alexander grabbed the keys. "We should search her car for clues!"

Alexander, Rip, and Nikki raced down to the lobby, with Mr. Hoarsely trailing behind.

"Slow down!" shouted a short man with a big mustache.

It was Mr. Plunkett, Alexander's old teacher.

"Where are you goofballs off to in such a hurry?" asked Mr. Plunkett.

"Oh, um, uh —" stammered Mr. Hoarsely. "We're looking for —"

"Monsters!" said Rip, rolling his eyes. "They're all over town!"

"Ha! Good one!" said Mr. Plunkett. "You crack me up, Bonkowski." He continued on his way.

Mr. Hoarsely sighed. "It's a shame Mr. Plunkett can't see monsters anymore."

"*Anymore?*" asked Nikki, stopping in her tracks. "What do you mean?"

Rodney Plunkett was the third member of the original S.S.M.P. We were fighting a three-eyed something-or-other at his eighth birthday party.

That's when Rodney flipped, and the monster got away.

"Flipped?" asked Alexander.

"Yeah," said Mr. Hoarsely. "Nobody can see monsters after their eighth birthday."

"Like our friend Dottie!" said Alexander, his eyes widening. "As soon as she blew out her birthday candles, she stopped seeing monsters!"

"That's how it works," said Mr. Hoarsely. "But monsters can always see other monsters. Like Rip and Nikki — and Ms. Vanderpants."

"So how come *you* can still see monsters?" Rip asked.

Mr. Hoarsely sighed. "Beats me. Tomorrow's my thirty-second birthd —"

SQUEAK! Alexander skidded to a halt on the shiny floor. "Oh no!" He slapped his head.

"What is it, Salamander?" asked Nikki.

"Tomorrow is *my* birthday," said Alexander. "My *eighth* birthday!"

CHAPTER 5 GRAVEYARD SHIFT

Alexander looked as though someone had dropped a piano on his head. "I don't want to turn eight!" he said. "I can't leave the S.S.M.P.!"

"Snap out of it, weenie!" said Rip, shaking Alexander by the shoulders.

"Yeah! We've got a principal to rescue!" said Nikki.

Alexander nodded. "You're right. I need to stay focused."

Mr. Hoarsely led the three friends into the parking lot. He pointed to a clean, gray car.

"Have at it," he said. "If you need me, I'll be under my desk!" He sprinted back inside.

Alexander unlocked the car, and the S.S.M.P. started searching for clues. They found a lint brush, a magazine, and a strange drawing.

"Why did Vanderpants draw a bunch of bumps with my name on 'em?" asked Rip.

Nikki laughed. "Rip, those are gravestones. R.I.P. means 'Rest in Peace.' This drawing looks like it might be a map . . ."

24

"It *is* a map!" cried Alexander. "That graveyard is near the Gloamy Mountains! And look — Ms. Vanderpants circled one of the gravestones!"

"We need to find that grave!" said Rip.

The friends hiked across town.

By the time they reached the graveyard, the sky had turned as cold and gray as the gravestones at their feet.

"I'm starving!" said Rip.

"Me, too," said Alexander. "Let's eat before we look for that grave."

They plopped down for a picnic.

After lunch, they searched the graveyard. Heavy clouds were rolling fast overhead.

"Some of these gravestones look more like creepy statues," said Rip.

Nikki quickly found the grave marked on the map.

R.I.P.

ELMER MOOSELIDGE

HE LIVED LIFE SLOWLY
BUT DIED SO MUCH SPEEDIER
WHEN HIS FACTORY
WAS HIT BY A METEOR

"Who was Elmer Mooselidge?" Alexander wondered aloud. "Why would Ms. Vander —"

GRUUNNNGCHH!!

Alexander didn't finish his sentence. The stone reptile head on the grave next to him had turned to look him in the eye.

6 REST IN PIECES

With a gravelly grunt, the monster swung its heavy tail.

PLOMFFFFF! The stone reptile smashed Elmer Mooselidge's gravestone into a million pebbles.

"It's a rockodile!" shouted Alexander. "Split up!"

The friends took off in different directions.

The rockodile turned in place like a board game spinner.

Its snout pointed to Alexander. Then it tromped after him, its jaws wide open.

"How do we beat this boulder-brain?!" shouted Rip, clambering up a tree.

PIT-PIT-PAT! Rain began to fall.

Alexander tried to remember the ROCKODILE pages of the notebook.

ROCKODILE

Stone reptile.

HABITAT
Surrounded by things made of stone.

DIET
Aquarium sand.

BEHAVIOR

Good news: This monster won't eat you with its powerful jaws! Bad news: Instead, it will grind you into gravel. Just for fun.

WHAM! The rockodile's sledgehammer tail can smash boulders.

FUN FACT! The rockodile got its name because it loves the electric guitar.

WARNING! You'd need heavy equipment—like a wrecking ball—to demolish a rockodile.

"We need a wrecking ball!" Alexander yelled.

CLOMP! The monster's powerful jaws snapped at Alexander's heels.

"How about a smashy-smashy monster?" yelled Rip.

"That could work!" Alexander called back. He ran left — then right. The rockodile's twisty body easily kept up, smashing graves along the way.

"I WILL SNAP YOU TO BITS!" roared the rockodile. Its voice sounded like two bricks scraping together. "JUST LIKE THE BOSS-MONSTER ORDERED!"

"You know the boss-monster?" Nikki asked, popping up from behind a grave. "That's just the creature we're looking for!"

The rain was falling harder now, and the ground was slippery with mud.

Nikki slipped and fell. The rockodile sprung toward her.

"Smashy smashy!" yelled Rip. He popped a chocolate-chunk cookie into his mouth, jumped down, and transformed before his boots hit the ground.

GRAWW-WWRRR-RRRR!!!

33

Monster-Rip charged at the rockodile.
The two monsters collided.

Monster-Rip slammed into the mud.

CRICCKCK! Cracks spread along the rockodile's body. Then the monster crumbled into pieces.

Rip sat up, muddy and back-to-normal. "I did it!" he said. He hopped to his feet and gave himself a high five.

"That totally rocked!" Alexander shouted.

"Not *totally*," said Nikki. "We should've asked the rockodile about the boss-monster before Rip crushed it to rubble."

"We need to focus on Elmer Mooselidge," said Alexander. "Why did Ms. Vanderpants mark his grave? And —"

FLASH! A bolt of lightning split the sky.

"Yikes," said Alexander. "We should get home."

"See you bright and early tomorrow," said Nikki.

"Yeah, Salamander. We need to make your last day in the S.S.M.P. really count!" said Rip.

Alexander got home just in time for dinner.

"Hey, Dad," Alexander asked with a mouthful of peas. "Have you ever heard of someone named Elmer Mooselidge?"

"Hmm ... Mooselidge ..." his dad said. "Sounds familiar ..."

Alexander swallowed.

"Ah yes, there was something in my old rocket kit!" said his dad. He walked over to the closet and brought back a small, white bottle.

"Mooselidge Glue?" said Alexander.

"Yeah," said his dad. "There was a Mooselidge glue factory here in Stermont. It closed down years ago after some kind of freak accident — like an earthquake or a tornado."

The meteor! Alexander jumped up. "Excuse me, Dad!"

Alexander ran to his room. His old Stermont placemat maze was tucked into the frame of his dresser mirror. He traced his finger along the maze to an abandoned factory at the bottom left corner.

Ms. Vanderpants must have been interested in this old factory, thought Alexander. He looked at his 7-year-and-365-day-old face. *Was the rockodile my last monster battle, ever?* He sighed as he tucked the map into his backpack.

7 PLATE OF EIGHTS

Alexander woke up to the best of all possible morning smells: pancakes!

He got dressed and ran downstairs.

"Happy birthday, Al!" said his dad. "Let's start this date with a plate of eights!"

Figure-eight pancake

Eight blueberries

Eight strawberries

Eight ounces of orange juice

"Thanks, Dad," said Alexander, digging in.

"But wait! Here's the greatest eight of all!" His dad handed him a gift with eight bows.

Alexander tore into the gift.

"Dress socks?" He tried not to frown.

"Heck, yeah!" said his dad. "You're turning eight today. No more comics or action figures for you — big kids get *useful* gifts!"

"Uh, thanks," Alexander mumbled. He tossed the gift into his backpack.

"You're welcome!" his dad said. "Now get out there and have fun. I'll see you after school for your party!"

Alexander hurried outside to find Rip and Nikki waiting in his front yard.

"Birthday!" they said at the same time.

Alexander raised an eyebrow.

"We would have said 'happy birthday,'" Nikki explained, "but we're not super-happy about it."

"Thanks, guys," said Alexander. "Now let's get moving. While I'm still me."

"So, where to?" asked Rip. "School?"

"Not yet," said Alexander. "I figured out who Elmer Mooselidge is. I mean, was. He owned that old factory on the other side of town."

Alexander opened his placemat maze, and pointed to the abandoned glue factory.

Nikki's eyes widened. "Could that be the boss-monster's hideout?" she guessed.

"Only one way to find out!" said Rip.

8 THE GLUE FACTORY

Alexander, Rip, and Nikki hurried across town.

"The monsters are more active than ever!" said Nikki.

The three friends eventually reached the old abandoned glue factory.

"Whoa," said Nikki. "The factory's enormous!"

"And half the roof is smashed in," said Rip.

"I bet from the meteor," guessed Alexander.

The friends squeezed through a rusty gate and tiptoed around the outside of the building. The doors were padlocked, and the windows were boarded up.

"Hey — there's our way in," said Nikki.

Huge garage door

Long, deep scratches

Bite mark?

Open a crack

Alexander, Rip, and Nikki crawled inside on their bellies.

They found themselves in total darkness.

PLIP-PLIP! Water dripped from the ceiling.

"Jampire, what can you see?" asked Rip.

Nikki peered into the darkness. "Empty glue bottles and junky old machines," she said. "But no sign of Ms. Vanderpants."

There was a colorful glow in the distance.

Alexander and Rip followed Nikki into an enormous room. Rusty metal beams stretched up to the ceiling. Huge vats of glue lined one wall.

The last vat pulsed with an eerie rainbow glow.

"You guys?" said Alexander. "Why is the sparkle glue glowing?"

"Alexander Bopp?! Is that you?" whispered a familiar voice from above.

Alexander looked up, and gasped.

SCHOOL
GLUE

SOOPER-
DOOPER
GLUE

FLYTRAP
GLUE

RUBBER CEMENT
(QUICK-DRYING!)

Principal Vanderpants had been stuck to a steel beam with a glob of rubber cement.

"What are you doing here?!" she demanded.

"We came to rescue you!" yelled Rip.

"Oh, Ripley," said Ms. Vanderpants with a sigh. "Now who's going to rescue *you*?"

BWAAAAR-HAWR-HAWR!!! A horrible laugh echoed through the factory.

Just then, a huge green monster jumped out from behind the glowing vat.

SPARKLE
GLUE

CHAPTER 9 STICKY SITUATION

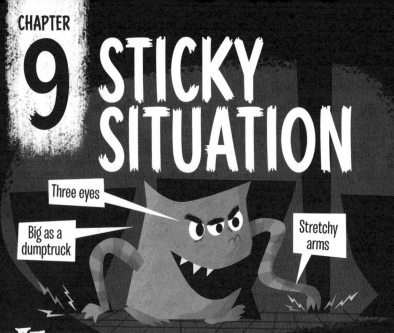

Three eyes

Big as a dumptruck

Stretchy arms

Hello, S.S.M.P.! I'm the boss-monster. Nice to *eat* you!"

The boss-monster's claws screeched against the metal floor as she moved toward Alexander, Rip, and Nikki.

"I remember this monster from the notebook!" said Alexander. "The three-eyed gloomp!"

"That's me!" said the gloomp. "And Helen Vanderpants was the perfect bait. I just love how the S.S.M.P. always sticks together!"

The monster lifted the RUBBER
CEMENT vat into the air.

Alexander, Rip, and Nikki
stepped backward, but there
was nowhere for them to go.
They were huddled under
Ms. Vanderpants's beam.

The gloomp's arms stretched back like rubber
bands, and — **PWING!** The
monster launched the vat
across the room.

BLORP! The vat smashed
into the steel beam. Glops
of rubber cement splattered all over Alexander,
Rip, and Nikki.

"Ugh!" said Rip. "It's gooey!"

Seconds later, the glue hardened. The S.S.M.P.
was cemented in place —
just like their principal.

"What do you want, boss-
monster?" asked Alexander.

"To take over Stermont once and for all — duh!" said the gloomp. "Which is why I've been making so many monsters."

"Wait — *making* monsters?!" said Nikki. "What do you mean?"

The boss-monster grinned from ear to pointy ear. "See how the SPARKLE GLUE vat is directly under the smashed-up part of the roof?"

"Yes . . ." said Nikki.

"Ohhhh!" said Alexander. "When the meteor hit the factory, it did something to that glue!"

"Correct," said the gloomp. "It gave the glue special powers. And I'm so glad I discovered them. Allow me to demonstrate."

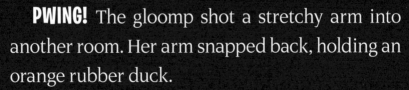

PWING! The gloomp shot a stretchy arm into another room. Her arm snapped back, holding an orange rubber duck.

"A weenie bath toy?" asked Rip.

"Just watch," said the gloomp.
"When it touches the sparkle glue . . ."

The boss-monster tossed the duck
into the glowing vat.

GALOORP-GLOP! The glue shimmered, casting
disco-ball sparkles around the room.

Then — **SQUACK!** A large, angry duck-monster
hopped out. It opened its toothy bill and sang a
squeaky song.

SQUEEKITY-
SQUABBITY-
SQUOOO!

Alexander felt tears well up in his eyes.

"Why are we crying?" sniffled Rip.

"It's a blubber duckie!" cried Alexander.

"Yep," said the gloomp, patting the duckie's
head. "Anything that hits this glue becomes
a monster. Throw in a fork and a porcupine?
Blammo! You've got a forkupine!"

"So wait," said Nikki. "Did you create *all* the monsters in Stermont?"

"Not all of them," said the gloomp. "I was a plain old everyday monster at first. Then one day I told a trample hamster to flatten an ice cream truck, and he *did!* That's when I realized my TRUE power: bossing other monsters around!"

The three-eyed gloomp sneered at Ms. Vanderpants. "But I should thank *you* most of all — for creating my recipe book."

PWING! The monster's arm shot over to a hole in the wall.

"Recipe book?" asked Ms. Vanderpants.

"Yes!" said the boss-monster. "The book *you* created! It describes every monster in Stermont!"

The gloomp's arm snapped back, holding a beat-up notebook with a skull on the cover.

Alexander gasped.

"Duckie — get them!" ordered the gloomp.

The blubber duckie waddled toward the monster-fighters, who were still stuck in place.

"Ha!" Rip snorted. "One monster can't stop us!"

The gloomp's eyes narrowed. "You think I've only made *one*?" She reached for the light switch.

KER-CLICK!

The factory lit up. The S.S.M.P. — old and new — was surrounded by grinning monsters.

CHAPTER

10 A LOSING BATTLE

Monsters crawled, hopped, flapped, slithered, shimmied, and lurched toward the S.S.M.P.

Alexander, Rip, and Nikki squirmed against the crusty rubber cement holding them to Ms. Vanderpants's beam.

"I know we can handle a few monsters at a time," said Nikki, "but there are *dozens* of monsters here."

"HUNDREDS!" hissed the gloomp. The boss-monster flipped through the notebook. "Spewnicorn, haircrow, frog-gobbler . . . They're all here! Ready to attack on my order."

"You're not the only monster who can give orders!" said Rip. He made three loud clicks with his tongue.

A few ants crawled out of his pocket.

Rip tossed candy to the ants.

BA-DINK! BA-DINK! As they ate it, the ants grew into huge, blue, puppy-sized bugs.

The three gi-norm-ants bowed down to Rip. Then they skittered around, chewing the rubber cement holding the friends in place.

"I love a good fight," said the boss-monster, fanning herself with the notebook. "Especially when it's a zillion versus four. Plus a few ants, I guess."

CRUNCH! Alexander broke free from the cement. He helped pull Rip and Nikki out, while the ants skittered up the beam toward Ms. Vanderpants.

"ATTACK!" screamed the gloomp.

HROOAOOOOOAAARRRRR!!!

The swarm of monsters obeyed their boss.

Rip punched a honkflower, Nikki chopped a giant onion, and Alexander slide-tackled a skunky-monkey. The gi-norm-ants stopped chomping at Ms. Vanderpants's glue and joined the fight.

SNARL! OOF! AWWWK! BLOOMP! MEOW! BLARFF! The room was a blur of feathers, scales, claws, fur, and snouts. Alexander couldn't tell where one monster ended and the next began.

BLOING! A yak-in-the-box sprung open, flinging Alexander high above the battle. In mid-air, he caught a glimpse of Rip tripping a barfalo and of Nikki swatting a skeeter-copter.

There are too many monsters, thought Alexander. *We're losing . . . BADLY.*

BWAAR-HAWR-HAWR!!! The boss-monster laughed, with one eye on each member of the S.S.M.P.

"Urf!" Alexander landed on the back of a rhinoceraptor.

"Bring him to me!" the boss-monster commanded.

The rhino-bird dive-bombed a nearby crate. **WHAM!** Alexander was bucked in the air — straight into the gloomp's waiting claws.

SOCK IT TO 'EM

The boss-monster dangled Alexander upside-down over her open mouth.

"Noooo!" Rip and Nikki shouted. They ran toward the gloomp but were blocked by a flock of cutterflies.

Alexander twisted to try and free himself from the monster's grasp. As he squirmed, he heard a crinkling noise.

My gift . . . he thought.

Alexander unzipped his backpack. Some party invitations fluttered to the floor. He reached in and yanked out his dress socks.

The gloomp used her free arm to pick up an invitation.

"What have we here?" she asked. "You're having a party? Thanks for inviting me! I loooove birthday cake."

While the boss-monster was going on about cake, Alexander tossed all eight socks into the sparkle glue.

SPARKLE GLUE

GALOOORP-GLOP! The glue shimmered, casting disco-ball sparkles around the room.

"Huh?" said the gloomp, with a toothy frown.

A brand-new monster flopped out of the vat. A spinning, growling socktopus, the size of a carnival ride.

SOCKTOPUS
Woven monster made from eight mismatched socks.

SNAP! FLAP! SNAP! The socktopus snapped its arms like whips. It immediately wrapped itself around the boss-monster.

The gloomp tossed Alexander aside, and began wrestling the socktopus.

Socks really are a useful gift! Alexander thought, quickly backing away.

"LET! GO! OF! ME!" the boss-monster bossed in her bossiest voice.

The socktopus obeyed. It stretched out in eight directions and became tangled in the beams holding up the ceiling.

CRACK! Ms. Vanderpants's beam bent in half.

"Uh-oh," said the gloomp.

Bricks fell from the ceiling, hitting monsters on their shells, wings, and tails.

Alexander, Rip, and Nikki jumped out of the way.

"Well done, Alexander!" said Ms. Vanderpants. She wriggled against the bent beam and transformed into a nar-madillo. The beam fell like a tree, pinning the boss-monster to the floor.

"OOF!" The gloomp dropped the notebook. Quick as a ninja, Nikki grabbed it.

"You rule, Nikki!" cheered Alexander.

A huge section of wall caved in. Sunlight streamed into the factory.

"The whole place is falling apart!" Rip shouted.

"You have the notebook — for now!" the boss-monster roared. "But I will see you tonight — at your weirdo party!" The gloomp wadded up the invitation and swallowed it.

"Follow me, students!" said Ms. Vanderpants. She tucked into a ball. Then she barreled through the wall. Alexander, Rip, and Nikki dove after her.

A half second later, the entire glue factory collapsed.

12 NEED A LIFT?

"Climb onto that forklift!" shouted Ms. Vanderpants. She pointed to a broken-down piece of machinery in the weedy parking lot. "We need to leave — FAST! That collapsed factory won't hold the monsters for long!"

Alexander, Rip, and Nikki squeezed into the forklift's seat as the army of monsters began rising from the rubble.

"I'll power this thing," said Ms. Vanderpants. "Ripley, you steer."

"Woo-hoo!" Rip shouted. "Wait — where are we going?"

"To school," said Ms. Vanderpants. "It's 4:00, so the students should all be gone."

Four o'clock?! thought Alexander. *Less than an hour until I turn eight!*

Ms. Vanderpants crouched down and began spinning like a ball. She rolled against the forklift and ball-spun it forward at rocket speed.

Alexander and Nikki held on tight as Rip steered the forklift over sidewalks, through a fountain, and across downtown Stermont.

By 4:03, the forklift skidded to a stop, right in front of Stermont Elementary.

"Excellent work, Ripley Bonkowski," said Ms. Vanderpants. "Now, everyone inside!"

The S.S.M.P. ran into the lobby. Alexander could hear the rumbling of a monster stampede in the distance.

"We shouldn't have come here!" said Nikki. "We've led the monsters straight to our brand-new school!"

Ms. Vanderpants smiled. "This isn't a school. It's a fortress."

Seconds later, a wave of monsters smashed through the doors. Ms. Vanderpants flipped a switch on the side of a water fountain.

Spiky cement balls dropped from the ceiling, crushing the monsters.

"Amazing!" Rip cheered. "You bowled five strikes, all at once!"

"This way — hurry!" said Ms. Vanderpants. She twisted a fire extinguisher. **VRRT!** A hidden panel slid open, revealing an elevator.

"Awesome!" said Nikki.

There was only one button in the secret elevator. Ms. Vanderpants pressed it with her horn.

On the ride up, the S.S.M.P. peppered their principal with questions.

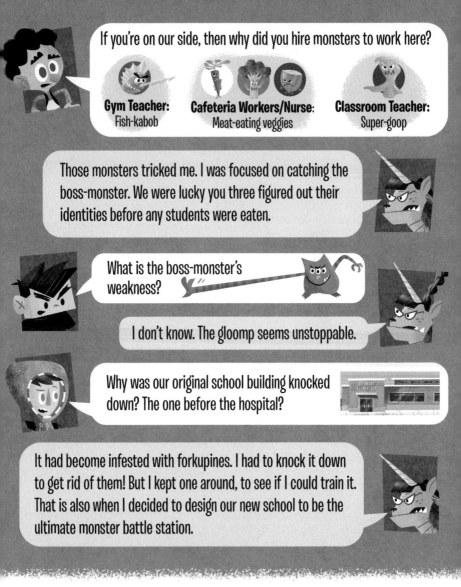

If you're on our side, then why did you hire monsters to work here?

Gym Teacher: Fish-kabob

Cafeteria Workers/Nurse: Meat-eating veggies

Classroom Teacher: Super-goop

Those monsters tricked me. I was focused on catching the boss-monster. We were lucky you three figured out their identities before any students were eaten.

What is the boss-monster's weakness?

I don't know. The gloomp seems unstoppable.

Why was our original school building knocked down? The one before the hospital?

It had become infested with forkupines. I had to knock it down to get rid of them! But I kept one around, to see if I could train it. That is also when I decided to design our new school to be the ultimate monster battle station.

DING! The elevator doors slid open. The S.S.M.P. found themselves in the principal's office.

68

13 STERMONT ELEMENTARY

BATTLE ^ STATION!

"Eep!" Mr. Hoarsely jumped up from beneath the principal's desk. "You're alive!"

He squeezed Ms. Vanderpants.

"No time for hugs," said Ms. Vanderpants. "We must activate the battle stations. Would you enter the code?"

Mr. Hoarsely typed into a control panel on the desk.

VWOOOP! VWOOOP!

Screens and electronic gizmos dropped down from the ceiling.

The radar map lit up with dots. Monsters appeared on every screen.

TODAY'S MENU
...DAY: Texas toast
TUESDAY: Baked Alaska
WEDNESDAY: Turkey Manhattan
THURSDAY: Boston beans
FRIDAY: Stermont Stew

CAFETERIA

GYM

"That chill-billy has already destroyed the cafeteria!" cried Nikki.

Ms. Vanderpants stepped forward. "I designed this building to fight every kind of monster." She pointed to a screen labeled GYM. "See that balloon goon?"

Alexander could see a balloon goon sucking the air out of basketballs.

Ms. Vanderpants held a silver bell up to a microphone. **LING-A-LING-A-LING!**

A moment later, a forkupine spun into the room, scratching up the gym floor.

"*This* is what I have been training him for!" said Ms. Vanderpants.

The goon frowned when it saw the poky monster. The forkupine leapt onto the goon, bursting it instantly. **BLAM!**

"Pop goes the monster!" cheered Rip.

"Now find your battle station!" shouted Ms. Vanderpants.

BATTLE STATIONS

STERMONT ELEMENTARY

RIP
1. Planetarium light-cannon.
(Not just a star show!) Blasts
any monster that hates light.

NIKKI
2. Gym floor-waxer.
Mops up dirty, stinky monsters.

MR. HOARSELY
3. In charge of snacks.

MS. VANDERPANTS
**4. Heavy-duty apple-peeler
in the kitchen.**
Shreds plant and veggie monsters.

5. Paint mixer in the art room.
Shakes the shells off armored monsters.

**6. Laser-guided pencil
sharpeners in the library.**
(All-purpose attack!)

"Where's my station?" asked Alexander.

Ms. Vanderpants — for the first time Alexander could remember — laughed. "You, Mr. Bopp, are in charge. This is what you've been training for. To lead the S.S.M.P.'s biggest battle EVER!"

"You'll need this, Salamander," said Nikki. She pulled the notebook from her hoodie pocket, and tossed it to her friend.

Alexander's heart leapt. It felt good to have the notebook back . . . like a missing part of him had been returned. He flipped it open and started calling out commands to his team.

"Rip! Blind that blinker!"

"Nikki! Soak that trash-squatch!"

"Ms. Vanderpants! Bash that bumble-beaver!"

"Careful — we've got pool sharks in the toilets! A rust-buster is swallowing saxophones in the music room! Oh, and there's a megaworm in the courtyard!"

Before long, the S.S.M.P. had defeated every monster in the school.

"Hooray!" Mr. Hoarsely threw his arms — and a dozen crackers — into the air. "We beat the boss-monster's army!"

"But wait!" Rip yelled. "Where is the boss?"

"Oh no," said Alexander, digging inside his backpack. "I know exactly where she is." With a shaky hand, he held up an invitation to the weirdest party ever.

CHAPTER 14
ALEXANDER'S WISH

Alexander! Go protect your father from the gloomp!" said Ms. Vanderpants. "Mr. Hoarsely will drive you three home, while I do a quick sweep of the school for hidden monsters."

Mr. Hoarsely's hair turned a shade whiter. "What?! No way!" he said. "I just got you back, Ms. Vanderpants! I'm never leaving your side again!"

"Sheesh! I'll drive!" said Rip. "I already drove once today. It's easy."

Everyone looked at Ms. Vanderpants.

She sighed, shrugged, and tossed Rip a set of keys.

A minute later, Rip was behind the wheel of the school bus. He stood on the gas pedal all the way to Alexander's house.

SCREEEEEECCCH! The tires squealed as Rip slammed on the breaks. The bus stopped in Alexander's driveway. At least, *one* wheel was in the driveway.

"Everybody out!" said Rip. He opened the bus doors.

"Dad! Where are you?" called Alexander, jumping off the bus.

The three friends raced inside the house.

"SURPRISE!" yelled Alexander's dad as he jumped out of a closet.

Alexander looked around. No sign of the gloomp — yet.

"Dad!" he shouted, and bear-hugged his dad. "Are you alright?"

"Sure I am, kiddo!" said his dad. "It's cake time! And your timing is perfect! 4:56 — two minutes until your actual birthday!" He turned off the lights and ran into the kitchen to get the cake.

Alexander looked at Rip and Nikki.

"I guess this is good-bye," said Nikki.

"If you can't *see* monsters anymore, will you also *forget* everything you know about monsters?" asked Rip. "Will you remember that Nikki likes strawberry gummies?"

"Or that Rip likes to smash stuff?" added Nikki.

"I don't know," said Alexander. "But I will remember that you're my two best friends." He gave Rip and Nikki a hug. "Good luck fighting the boss-monster. And, uh, don't get eaten."

Alexander's dad came in, carrying a birthday cake with eight glowing candles. He set it in front of Alexander. "Make a wish, Al!"

Alexander looked at Nikki. She smiled back, showing her fangs. He looked at Rip. Rip nodded. So did the ant on his shoulder.

Alexander made his wish.

The clock changed to 4:58 and he blew out his candles.

15 ONE ANGRY BOSS

Alexander blinked. *Am I supposed to feel dizzy or something?* he wondered.

GRORARRAAARRRR!!!!

A horrible sound came from out in the woods. Rip and Nikki jumped up. So did Alexander.

Alexander's dad whistled as he cut the cake.

"Salamander!" said Nikki. "You could hear that monster roar?"

"Yes!" said Alexander.

"But how is that possible?" asked Rip.

Alexander scratched his chin. "Do you think I'm a mon —"

GROOAARR!!! SMASH! CRASH!

"Let's move, weenies!" cried Rip. "We've got a boss to battle!"

The friends ran outside and tore through the woods.

The three-eyed gloomp was kicking, punching, and smashing the S.S.M.P.'s caboose.

KER-
BLASH!

"Hey! That's our headquarters!" Nikki shouted.

"Not anymore!" growled the gloomp. "You destroyed *my* hideout, so I destroyed yours! You can't possibly defeat me now that I've busted all your monster-fighting gear!"

"Not *all* our gear!" said Alexander. He held up the notebook. "If we could steal our book back from you — which is NOT a recipe book by the way — then we can do anything."

"You wish!" said the gloomp. "I am going to create a *new* army of monsters! Before the factory collapsed, I was able to save one last bottle of *this*!" The boss-monster held up a glowing squeeze bottle.

"The sparkle glue!" said Nikki. She turned to Rip and Alexander. "We can't let her use it!"

"Oh, I'll use it all right," said the boss-monster. "Right after I finally eat the three of you!"

The gloomp leaned forward and licked her lips. "Who's first?"

"I've got this, guys!" Rip shouted. He gobbled up a cookie, transformed, and charged at the gloomp.

The gloomp flicked Monster-Rip aside like a bug.

"Leave Rip alone!" cried Nikki. She pulled a broken hockey stick from the caboose wreckage. She leapt toward the gloomp.

But Nikki didn't swing her stick at the monster. Instead, she used it to slap-shot the squeeze bottle — **ZING!** — right into Alexander's hand.

POW! The gloomp knocked Nikki back.

"HEY!" roared the gloomp. "NO ONE STEALS FROM THE BOSS-MONSTER!"

The boss-monster's long bungee-arms shot out. Alexander, Rip, and Nikki were surrounded.

The gloomp's scaly arms closed in on all sides.

"Well, you're not the boss of *us*," said Alexander. He held the squeeze bottle over the notebook, and turned it upside down.

"Salamander!" cried Nikki. "What are you doing?"

"Stop!" yelled Rip. "You'll ruin the notebook!"

"It's the only way!" Alexander said.

He squeezed the bottle. **SPLORT!** Rainbow sparkle glue splattered all over the notebook.

CHAPTER 16 NOTEBOOK OF DOOM

GALOOOOORP-GLOP! The notebook shimmered, casting disco-ball sparkles around the woods.

Alexander tossed it to the ground, careful not to touch the glue.

The monster notebook flapped around. Its spine cracked. The pages grew larger, folding into horns and eyes and wings and claws.

"It's like — an origami monster!" said Nikki, taking a step back.

RAOOOOOARR! The notebook sprouted into a humongous monster. Larger than anything the S.S.M.P. had ever seen.

"Ummm, Salamander?" said Rip. "Maybe that wasn't your best idea."

Alexander, Rip, and Nikki all backed away from the towering doom-monster.

"Thank you, Alexander Bopp," said the boss-monster.

"For what?" asked Alexander.

"For creating the perfect minion for me to boss around. Just look at those heads! And those claws! And I looooove the smell of old books."

The gloomp stepped forward and shouted at the doom-monster. "I ORDER YOU TO DESTROY THE SUPER SECRET MONSTER PATROL!"

But instead of attacking the S.S.M.P., the doom-monster leaned down — **GULP!** — and swallowed the gloomp.

"Uh-oh," said Nikki.

"What now?" asked Rip.

"Hooray?" guessed Alexander.

One of the doom-monster's heads glared down at them, angrily. But the rest of the heads looked a little sick.

"Uh, guys?" said Rip. "That's how I look when I eat my grandpa's chili."

The monster blinked. It hiccupped. It made gurgling sounds. Then —

KERR-PLOOOOMIE!!

The doom-monster burped an earth-shattering burp, and its monstrous origami body exploded. Shreds of paper rained down all over Stermont.

Alexander, Rip, and Nikki smiled, laughed, and danced in the falling confetti.

"Who wants cake?" asked Alexander. He led his friends back to his house.

"There you are!" said Alexander's dad, standing in their backyard. "Look who else came to your party: Ms. Vanderpants! And Mr. Hoarsely! Did you know it's *his* birthday, too?"

"Wait, really?" asked Alexander.

"Yeah," said Mr. Hoarsley. "I have a weird leap-day birthday, just like you. Except I turn thirty-two today!"

"Thirty-two?" Nikki repeated.

"Wait a minute . . . That's it!" cried Alexander. His eyes grew wide. "Leap year only comes around once every FOUR years!"

"That means today is . . ." said Rip, counting on his knuckles, "Hoarsely's eighth birthday!"

MR. HOARSELY'S AGE IN LEAP YEARS

= 32 years old today!

"Oh!" said Alexander's dad. "Mr. Hoarsely should make a wish, too!" He plopped a fresh candle on a slice of cake. Then he lit the candle and passed the cake to Mr. Hoarsely.

Mr. Hoarsely blew out his candle. Then he sat back in his chair and smiled. His hair had gone black again.

"I'll get the ice cream," said Alexander's dad, heading to the kitchen.

"This is GREAT news, Salamander!" said Nikki. "This leap-day loophole means you'll be able to lead the S.S.M.P. for years to come."

"Yup, today's only my *second* birthday!" said Alexander.

"But wait," said Rip. "We beat the boss-monster. Does that mean we're done? Fighting monsters, I mean?"

Ms. Vanderpants took a bite of cake and pursed her lips. "I'm afraid your work will never be done," she said. "New googly-eyed monsters will show up, all covered with ooze, trying to swallow school children whole."

"Then we swear that we'll fight 'em!" said Rip.

"And try not to lose!" added Nikki.

"By leading this Secret Patrol," finished Alexander.

That night, after everyone had gone home, Alexander looked at himself in the mirror. He saw a tired pile of bones.

Actually, the bones weren't in a pile. They made up a strong skeleton, which was filled with guts. On top of that skeleton sat a huge skull with a pair of warm, bright eyes.

The whole thing was covered in a layer of skin, with a mop of curly hair on top. This mop-haired, bright-eyed, gutsy bag of bones was named Alexander Bopp. And he wasn't scared of anything. Not with brave, funny friends by his side.

TROY CUMMINGS

has no tail, no wings, no fangs, no claws, and only one head. As a kid, he believed that monsters might really exist. Today, he's sure of it.

BEHAVIOR This creature loves the feeling of snapping the last piece into a jigsaw puzzle. (Or the last monster into an early chapter book series!)

HABITAT A few cornfields west of Indianapolis.

DIET A baker's dozen of blueberry donuts. (Thirteen just seems like a nice number, doesn't it?)

EVIDENCE Few people believe that Troy Cummings is real. The only proof we have is that he supposedly wrote and illustrated The Eensy-Weensy Spider Freaks Out!, and Can I Be Your Dog?

WARNING Protect yourself by learning about every monster the S.S.M.P. has battled!

MONSTER NOTEBOOK